W9-BEG-566

1914

Rebecca
AND ANA

By JACQUELINE DEMBAR GREENE

ILLUSTRATIONS ROBERT HUNT

VIGNETTES SUSAN MCALILEY

★ American Girl®

THE AMERICAN GIRLS

1764

KAYA, an adventurous Nez Perce girl whose deep love for horses and respect for nature nourish her spirit

1774

FELICITY, a spunky, spritely colonial girl, full of energy and independence

1824

JOSEFINA, a Hispanic girl whose heart and hopes are as big as the New Mexico sky

1854

KIRSTEN, a pioneer girl of strength and spirit who settles on the frontier

1864

ADDY, a courageous girl determined to be free in the midst of the Civil War

1904   SAMANTHA, a bright Victorian beauty, an orphan raised by her wealthy grandmother

1914   REBECCA, a lively girl with dramatic flair growing up in New York City

1934   KIT, a clever, resourceful girl facing the Great Depression with spirit and determination

1944   MOLLY, who schemes and dreams on the home front during World War Two

1974   JULIE, a fun-loving girl from San Francisco who faces big changes—and creates a few of her own

Published by American Girl Publishing
Copyright © 2009 by American Girl

All rights reserved. No part of this book may be used or reproduced in
any manner whatsoever without written permission except in the case of
brief quotations embodied in critical articles and reviews.

Questions or comments? Call 1-800-845-0005, visit **americangirl.com**,
or write to Customer Service, American Girl, 8400 Fairway Place,
Middleton, WI 53562-0497.

Printed in China
13 14 15 16 17 LEO 10 9 8 7 6 5

All American Girl marks, Rebecca™, Rebecca Rubin™, and Ana™
are trademarks of American Girl.

PICTURE CREDITS
The following individuals and organizations have generously given
permission to reprint images contained in "Looking Back":
p. 2—the Western Union name, logo, and related trademarks and service marks, owned by
Western Union Holdings Inc., are registered and/or used in the U.S. and many foreign countries;
pp. 72–73—Brown Brothers (classroom; hygiene inspection); P.S. 97 report card, February 1920,
Museum of the City of New York, gift of Ruth Orr Kebles (01.5.2A); Library of Congress
(bathhouse); pp. 74–75—Brown Brothers (rooftop recess); © Lake County Museum/Corbis
(nursery school); pp. 76–77—George Eastman House (factory girl; street scene);
Brown Brothers (newsboy); © Rykoff Collection/Corbis (family)

Library of Congress Cataloging-in-Publication Data

Greene, Jacqueline Dembar.
Rebecca and Ana / by Jacqueline Dembar Greene ;
illustrations, Robert Hunt ; vignettes, Susan McAliley.
p. cm.
Summary: Nine-year-old Rebecca Rubin eagerly helps her cousin Ana, newly arrived from
Russia, to adjust to life in New York City, but when their teacher says the two must sing
together at a school assembly, Rebecca worries that her big moment will be ruined.
ISBN 978-1-59369-522-4 (pbk.) — ISBN 978-1-59369-523-1 (hardcover)
1. Jews—New York (State)—New York—Juvenile fiction. [1. Jews—United States—Fiction.
2. Immigrants—Fiction. 3. Cousins—Fiction. 4. Schools—Fiction.
5. Family life—New York (State)—New York—Fiction.
6. New York (N.Y.)—History—20th century—Fiction.]
I. Hunt, Robert, 1952–, ill. II. McAliley, Susan, ill. III. Title.
PZ7.G834Reb 2009   [Fic]—dc22   2009017757

TO MY GREAT-GRANDPARENTS,
MAX AND YETTA WEBBER,
WHO BRAVELY LEFT DVINSK, RUSSIA,
TO MAKE A NEW LIFE IN AMERICA

Rebecca's parents and grandparents came to America before
Rebecca was born, along with
millions of other Jewish immigrants
from different parts of the world.
These immigrants brought with them
many different traditions and ways
of being Jewish. Practices varied
widely between families, and differ-
ences among Jewish families were
just as common in Rebecca's time as
they are today. Rebecca's stories
show the way one Jewish family
could have lived in 1914 and 1915.

Rebecca's grandparents spoke
mostly *Yiddish,* a language that was
common among Jews from Eastern
Europe. For help in pronouncing or
understanding the foreign words
in this book, look in the glossary on
page 78.

TABLE OF CONTENTS

REBECCA'S FAMILY AND FRIENDS

CHAPTER ONE
WELCOME TO AMERICA   1

CHAPTER TWO
A YIDDISH MISTAKE   16

CHAPTER THREE
MUSIC FOR A SONG   34

CHAPTER FOUR
TWO SONGBIRDS   43

CHAPTER FIVE
A NEW FLAG WAVES   55

LOOKING BACK   71

GLOSSARY   78

A SNEAK PEEK AT
CANDLELIGHT FOR REBECCA   79

REBECCA'S FAMILY

PAPA
Rebecca's father, an understanding man who owns a small shoe store

MAMA
Rebecca's mother, who keeps a good Jewish home—and a good sense of humor

REBECCA
A lively girl who dreams of becoming an actress

SADIE AND SOPHIE
Rebecca's twin sisters, who like to remind Rebecca that they are fourteen

BENNY AND VICTOR
Rebecca's brothers, who are five and twelve

. . . AND FRIENDS

UNCLE JACOB
Ana's father, who has brought his family all the way from Russia

AUNT FANNIE
Ana's mother, who hopes for a better life for her family in America

ANA
Rebecca's nine-year-old cousin, who is learning to speak English

JOSEF AND MICHAEL
Rebecca's cousins, who are fifteen and thirteen

ROSE
A girl in Rebecca's class who knows what it's like to be an immigrant

CHAPTER
ONE

WELCOME TO AMERICA

 Rebecca squinted through the gray fog that blanketed New York Harbor. She could barely see the outline of the brick buildings at Ellis Island. That was where immigrants came when they first arrived in New York.

Papa was there now, meeting Uncle Jacob and his family. Papa had saved for months to buy ship tickets to bring them from Russia. Rebecca had helped by selling her needlework at Papa's shoe store. She knew the money she had earned wasn't even enough to pay for one ticket, but she liked feeling that she had at least helped bring over her cousin Ana.

Rebecca had worried about Ana ever since Uncle Jacob's telegram arrived a few weeks ago.

1

Escaped Russia with great difficulty.
Arriving New York 8 November 1914.

Ana had been ill before she left Russia. Was her health the "great difficulty" Uncle Jacob had mentioned?

If only Ana survived the journey safely, Rebecca was sure they would become as close as sisters. As the wind began to scatter the thin gray wisps of fog, she saw a small ferryboat chugging across the harbor. Behind it, the Statue of Liberty stood out against the clouds.

"Do you think Ana's on that ferry?" she asked, turning to her family. "We've been waiting for hours."

Rebecca's grandparents huddled together against the wind. Bubbie drew her kerchief tighter around her head, and Grandpa pulled his scarf up around his neck. Rebecca's little brother, Benny, stood on a bench, watching the boats. Her older brother, Victor, held on to Benny's collar so that he wouldn't tumble over.

"It takes a long time to get through Immigration," Mama told Rebecca.

Grandpa shook his head, remembering. "So many

people! Such lines! We shuffled into line to get off the ship. We stood in line to go into the building, *schlepping* everything we owned. Then another line while we walked up those steep stairs, praying nobody thought we looked sick."

"I should think *everyone* would feel sick after two weeks sailing across the ocean," said Rebecca's sister Sadie.

Sadie's twin, Sophie, looked sympathetically at her grandparents. "You must have been so anxious."

Bubbie nodded. "If inspectors thought something was wrong, they might not let us into America."

"When we were on the ship," Mama said, "other passengers warned us about passing through Immigration. Just because you land in New York, it doesn't mean you can live here. The officials keep out anyone who has a serious illness. If they think you have a problem, they mark a letter on your coat with chalk. An *E* means you might have an eye disease. *H* means you might have a heart problem. There's a long list."

Rebecca had heard lots of stories about Ellis Island from her friends at school. When immigrants had a disease that could spread, officials sent them back to the country they came from.

Rebecca remembered what her friend Rose Krensky had told her about immigrants who were sick when they arrived. "*Contagious disease*, they call it," Rose said. "You got one, you go back. That's it. And the ship company has to pay for your ticket." Rebecca tried to forget about Rose's words. She could only hope Ana was well enough to climb the stairs at Ellis Island.

Mama's cousin Max paced along the walkway. Now that he was an actor with a movie company, he had helped pay for the tickets, too. "I've got an idea," Max said, flashing his sparkling smile. "Let's practice a little welcoming song to greet the family when they step off the ferry. We'll sing 'You're a Grand Old Flag.'" He started humming.

"I know some of it," Rebecca said. "I heard it on the phonograph at the candy store."

"She buys one soda," Victor teased, "and hangs around for an hour, sucking up the music along with the drink!"

phonograph

4

Max started singing softly. Rebecca knew the chorus, and so did the twins. Her sisters linked their arms as they chimed in. "You're a grand old flag, you're a high-flying flag, and forever in peace may you wave . . ."

When Rebecca no longer knew the words, she hummed along. She listened carefully as Max sang. He made every word sound exciting! "You're the emblem of the land I love, the home of the *free* and the *brave* . . ." He emphasized some of the words, giving the song more rhythm. Bubbie nodded in time to the music, and Grandpa tapped his foot. Benny marched around them in a small circle, saluting every time he passed Max.

A loud horn blast whistled through the air, and Benny covered his ears. The ferry pulled up to the dock, smoke belching from its smokestack. Rebecca stretched up on her toes, trying to see the passengers on deck. Hundreds of people crowded at the railing in strange-looking clothing—rough black coats, long scarves that fell past their knees, odd flat caps and summer straw hats. Their arms were weighed down with feather beds, quilts, and bulging carpetbags, yet their tired faces glowed with excitement.

"Another boatload of new Americans," Max smiled. He nudged Mama. "Just like we were, not so long ago."

"There's Papa!" Rebecca exclaimed. She jumped up and down, waving in his direction. Papa had gone to Ellis Island to sign papers proving that Uncle Jacob and his family had someone to help them settle in America. Rebecca searched the crowd anxiously, trying to guess which girl was her cousin. Even if Ana was sick, the immigration officials wouldn't send her back to Russia alone, would they?

"Start singing," Max directed them.

Above the din of shuffling feet and shouted greetings in many languages, Rebecca sang with all her might.

"Over here!" Mama called, and Rebecca saw Papa standing next to his brother. Rebecca thought she would have recognized Uncle Jacob anywhere. Although he looked older than Papa, with streaks of gray in his hair and beard, he looked very much like her father. Beside him, Aunt Fanya looked pale and weary. Her shoulders slumped, and her eyes were

rimmed with dark circles. A boy a bit taller than Victor waved his hand toward them. He must be either Michael or Josef.

Then Rebecca saw a girl about her own age, right behind Aunt Fanya. It had to be Ana, but she looked nothing like Rebecca had imagined. Her cheeks were smudged with streaks of dirt. Her face looked thin and drawn under her wool scarf, but the rest of her bulged, and her clothes pulled at their buttons. Like the other immigrants, she had a large passenger tag pinned to her coat, which flapped in the breeze.

Rebecca glanced at the crowd behind them. Where was Ana's other brother? Perhaps he was further back in the crush of people.

Suddenly Max's voice trailed off. The musical greeting floated away as the families embraced each other.

"Thank heavens you're here!" Mama said as she hugged Aunt Fanya. Then she looked anxiously at the rest of the family. "Where is—?"

In Yiddish, Aunt Fanya cried, "They've taken Josef!" She began to sob, louder and louder until she was wailing. Strangers paused to look and then quickly turned away. Uncle Jacob put his arm around her shoulders, as if holding her up. Ana clutched her mother's arm and began to cry.

"Josef fell on the ship and hurt his leg badly," Papa explained. "He was limping when he passed through the inspection point, and the officials marked his coat with an *L*. They separated him from the others and took him away."

It didn't seem possible. Rebecca had worried about Ana making the voyage safely, but she had never imagined that someone else in the family might become sick. Now the officials were holding

Josef on Ellis Island and might send him back to
Russia! She thought about the mark on Josef's coat.

"Does *L* mean 'limp'?" she asked Papa.

"It means 'lame.' The doctors are afraid Josef
won't be able to walk." A deep frown creased Papa's
forehead, but he tried to sound hopeful. He turned
to his brother and added in Yiddish, "We'll come
back tomorrow and see about getting Josef released.
If all goes well, the Ellis Island doctors can treat him
and he'll be better soon."

Aunt Fanya tugged weakly at Papa's arm.
"Don't let them send him back!" Her eyes were
filled with fear.

"Don't worry," Papa said gently. "I'll go to the
Hebrew Immigrant Aid Society. They'll know what
to do."

Rebecca offered Ana her handkerchief. "Don't
cry," she said in Yiddish. "Papa will help." But she
knew from what Rose had told her that getting Josef
through Immigration wouldn't be easy.

Mama took the ship tags off the family's
clothing, and they all set off down the street, with
bundles clutched to their chests. Cousin Max held
Benny's hand and carried a big brass samovar under

one strong arm. Rebecca's family had a
samovar from Russia, too. Samovars were
used for making tea. Grandpa had always told
Rebecca that a samovar was a family's treasure
and something they tried not to leave behind.

samovar

Papa and Uncle Jacob carried a wicker
trunk between them. As they walked, Papa
explained how horseless trolleys worked.
Mama told Aunt Fanya about cooking on a gas
stove. Victor tried to explain the game of baseball to
Michael, batting at the air to demonstrate.

As always, the twins walked together, talking
and giggling, but for once, Rebecca didn't mind. She
usually hated it when her sisters left her out, but
now she had Ana by her side. She balanced a heavy
bundle against her chest and hooked her arm
through Ana's, pointing out a huge theater with
glittering lights.

"We have movies here," she said. "You
watch the actors moving on a screen instead
of on a stage." Ana's large brown eyes grew
wider. Rebecca had so much to share with
her cousin and could barely contain her
happiness now that she had arrived.

10

Although she was concerned about Josef, she was relieved that Ana's health was better. With fresh food from the markets, Ana would grow stronger every day. From now on, they would be together all the time.

When they entered their building, a cat dashed from the entrance down into the basement. "That's Pasta," Rebecca told Ana. "She belongs to Mr. Rossi, who takes care of the building. He says Pasta is the only cat who likes spaghetti more than chasing mice!"

Ana frowned. "Not know these words," she said. Before Rebecca could explain, Mama spoke.

"I know you all want baths," said Mama with a smile as they crowded into the apartment. "Louis," she said to Papa, "take your brother and Michael to the bath house." She handed Papa two towels, a small cake of soap, and a neatly tied bundle of fresh clothes. Then she pulled the metal washtub from under the sink and set it in the middle of the kitchen. She started filling a bucket with hot water.

"Hot water pours from the faucet?" Aunt Fanya marveled. "Right in the kitchen?"

Mama nodded. "The ladies will have their baths here. Everyone else, scoot!"

Bubbie herded the rest of the family upstairs. "I'll make tea," she said, "and I've got a big plate of *rugalach*." Max licked his lips.

Rebecca could wait until later for Bubbie's flaky cinnamon pastry. She wasn't going to leave Ana now. "I'll help with the baths," she announced.

rugalach

Ana untied her scarf, and Rebecca was delighted to see that her cousin's hair was the same rich brown shade as her own. They already looked almost like twins!

Layers of blouses, skirts, and sweaters lay beneath Ana's bulging buttons. By the time she had shed everything except her slip, Ana looked like a scrawny chicken that had lost all its feathers.

"We not have room to pack many things," Ana said in halting English. "I wear all clothes."

"How did you learn to speak English?" Rebecca asked. "You speak very well."

"In Russia, we have boarder who teach us English," Ana said proudly. "I learn fastly."

Mama looked doubtfully at the pile of dirty clothes. Rebecca knew that puffy peasant blouses and long skirts with bands of embroidery along the

By the time she had shed everything except her slip,
Ana looked like a scrawny chicken that had lost all its feathers.

hem would mark Ana as a *greenhorn*. That was the insulting term some Americans called newcomers just off the boat.

"Instead of washing these," Mama said, "I think you'll want to replace them with American clothes."

Aunt Fanya looked horrified. "Throw away clothes?"

Mama nodded. "I'm sure the ship was riddled with lice."

Rebecca shuddered at the thought of bugs crawling in her clothes. "I've got the perfect dress for Ana," she exclaimed. "In fact, with hand-me-downs from the twins, I've got two of everything! Ana and I can dress exactly alike."

"Now you're *Amerikanka*," Mama said to Fanya. "An American. The first thing to do is dress like one." She splashed a final bucket of hot water into the tub.

Ana stepped in and began scrubbing away weeks of grime and sour ship smells. "On ship, we must wash with salty seawater," she said. "Now water in tub is Ana soup!"

Rebecca laughed at the joke. Ana really did speak English pretty well. Rebecca sat down next to her aunt. "Now you should have an American name," she said. "May I call you Aunt Fannie?"

"Fannie," repeated her aunt. In Yiddish, she said, "I like this American name. I will dress American, and learn to speak it, too—if I stay." She twisted the fringes on her scarf and looked down sadly. "If Josef is sent back, we all go back together."

Ana stopped scrubbing, and her eyes brimmed with tears. "We can't go back to Russia," she said hoarsely. "It's too far. Papa can't work there, and Michael and Josef have to hide in the house from the tsar's soldiers."

Aunt Fannie began to cry, her shoulders shaking. Mama put her arms around her. "Even if there were enough money for new tickets," she said gently, "there's no life for you in Russia anymore." She looked steadily at Aunt Fannie. "I'm afraid there's no going back."

A cold feeling grew in Rebecca's stomach. The pile of clothes seemed like the Russian life Ana and her family had to throw away. But if Russia wasn't safe, how would Josef survive if he was sent back alone?

CHAPTER
TWO
—

A YIDDISH
MISTAKE

Rebecca felt warm and cozy in her
bed, and when she opened her eyes,
she remembered why. There was Ana,
sound asleep beside her, with Rebecca's wooden
doll, Beckie, smiling between them. *Now I've got a
twin, just like my sisters,* she thought happily. She
patted Ana's shoulder.

"Wake up," she said. "We're going to school!"
Ana stretched sleepily, kicking Rebecca's ankles, but
Rebecca didn't mind. "We can dress exactly alike,"
she announced. She pulled matching skirts and
sweaters from the closet and laid out stockings,
shoes, and hair ribbons. Rebecca helped her cousin
tie her stockings at her thighs.

"Don't be nervous about school," Rebecca said. "We're going to stay together the whole time." She brushed out her cousin's hair and tied on a fluffy bow. Then Ana did the same for her before they went into the kitchen.

"You two must think you're looking into a mirror," Mama exclaimed. "You look so alike, it's like having two sets of twins in the house!" Rebecca beamed, and Ana gave a shy smile.

Sadie urged Benny up from the chairs he slept on each night. Papa always pulled two chairs together for him and covered them with soft blankets. Now, every chair was needed at the table.

The apartment was crowded with the new family. Victor usually slept on the couch in the parlor, but he had let Michael take that spot. Instead, Victor had spent the night on a feather bed that Mama spread on the floor. Uncle Jacob and Aunt Fannie had slept upstairs in Bubbie and Grandpa's parlor, but they came down to help Michael and Ana go to school.

Mama set glasses of coffee mixed with milk on the table beside a heaping plate of sweet rolls.

"When Josef comes, we'll put another feather bed on the floor," she said.

If he comes, Rebecca thought.

Aunt Fannie looked at the coffee and rolls. "No tea?" she asked. "And what about soup?"

Rebecca giggled. "We don't have soup for breakfast in America! And we drink coffee in the morning." She stirred a lump of sugar into a glass of warm coffee milk and handed it to Ana.

After one sip, Ana smiled. "Is tasty!" she assured her mother. "America *is* land of milk and honey!"

As soon as one person finished eating, Mama washed the dishes and refilled them for someone else. Rebecca could barely move around the crowded kitchen, and there was no place for her to sit. As she stood near the warm stove eating her roll, there was a knock at the door. Papa opened it to find Mr. Rossi scowling at him.

"*Scusi*, Mr. Rubin," the janitor said, "but you know is against the rules to take in boarders here."

Papa appeared calm as he answered, but Rebecca saw his mustache twitch in anger. "Don't worry, Mr. Rossi, these aren't boarders. This is my brother and his family. They just got to America yesterday. They'll be getting settled on their own very soon." Papa smiled slightly. "You know how hard it is when you first arrive in New York!"

Mr. Rossi only grumbled. "A few days, okay, but no more. Otherwise, I have to report to the landlord. I come check again. I'm sorry, but it's my job." He left, and Papa closed the door.

"Where will we go?" Aunt Fannie asked, speaking in Yiddish.

"I'm going to start looking for a job today," Uncle Jacob said. "We don't want to cause trouble for you, Louis. I'm a good cabinet maker, and I hope to find work and a place to live as quickly as possible."

"You'll stay here as long as necessary," Papa reassured him. "If we have trouble with Mr. Rossi, I'll speak to the landlord myself."

"What a grouch," Rebecca said under her breath. Mr. Rossi always seemed to be griping about something. He even complained that Pasta didn't catch enough mice. Still, she couldn't help feeling a bit worried. Now he was causing trouble for Ana and her family. Rebecca had waited so long for Ana to arrive, and if Mr. Rossi made them move, she would lose her new twin. Mr. Rossi couldn't make them leave, could he?

Mama gave each of the children a lunch box and handed Aunt Fannie her scarf. "I'll help you register Michael and Ana at school," she said. "Be sure to bring their immigration papers along."

lunch box

Uncle Jacob patted his son on the head and beamed. "The best thing in America is free schools that everyone can attend," he said. "I hope Michael can keep going to school and not have to work."

"He's too young to have a job," Papa explained. "In New York, children must stay in school until they are fourteen years old."

Uncle Jacob sighed. "Thirteen or fourteen," he said, "makes no difference. If Josef can't help us earn a living, then Michael will have to work."

"Well, let's hope for the best," Papa said. He turned to Mama. "When you take Fanya to register the children, don't let the school put them with the first graders just because their English isn't perfect. They'll catch on quickly."

"Please make sure Ana stays in Miss Maloney's classroom with me," Rebecca pleaded. "Ana and

I are going to be like a new pair of shoes—always together!"

Outside, Mama and Aunt Fannie led the way, while Victor, Michael, and the girls followed in the brisk morning air. "Look, there's my friend Rose!" Rebecca said. "She moved here from Russia last year." They hurried to catch up, and Rebecca introduced her cousin.

Rose's hair was in tight braids, with a blue ribbon tied at the end of each one. "Ever been to school?" Rose asked Ana.

Ana shook her head. "At home my papa teaches me to read and figure numbers. But I'm speak English."

Rose wagged her finger in the air. "I'll give you a piece of advice. Don't speak a single word of Yiddish in school."

"Piece of advice?" Ana repeated. "Piece of paper, I know. Piece of bread, this I know. What is 'piece of advice'?"

"Oh, brother," Rose laughed. "You're going to have your hands full, Rebecca."

As the girls arrived at school, Ana hung back. "Is so big," she whispered, gazing up at the huge brick and stone building that nearly spanned a city block.

"Welcome to P.S. 64," Rebecca said. "The *P* stands for 'public,' which means everyone who lives here can attend for free. And the *S* just stands for 'school.'"

"In New York," Rose explained, "the neighborhood schools have numbers instead of names. We're lucky to go to P.S. 64, because it's nearly new."

Rebecca took Ana's hand and led her to the girls' entrance. "This is where we go in," she explained. "The boys have a different door. In the classroom there's a closet to hang up our things. You and I can share a hook."

Miss Maloney stood at the door, her hair in a puffy pompadour and her shirtwaist and skirt crisply pressed. Mama and Aunt Fannie waited politely to one side while the girls lined up.

"Silence, please," the teacher reminded the chattering girls. "Proceed into the school like young ladies."

Rebecca put her finger to her lips, and her cousin understood right away. Ana was smart, Rebecca thought, and would quickly catch on to the school routine.

As the girls filed in, Miss Maloney put her hand on Ana's shoulder. "And who are you?"

"That's my cousin," Rebecca explained. "She just came from Russia yesterday. She's exactly my age, Miss Maloney. I can help her if she stays with me."

The teacher looked uncertainly at Ana. "Your parents must register you at the office," she said. "You might belong in the class for immigrants who need to learn English."

Mama stepped forward and introduced herself and Aunt Fannie. "I'll help Mrs. Rubin with all the paperwork," she said, "and we expect Ana will do fine in a regular class, as long as Rebecca is nearby to help her out."

"I'm speak English," Ana declared. She cleared her throat. "My name is Ana Rubin. I have nine years. I can write English alphabet."

Miss Maloney crossed her arms and tapped her finger thoughtfully. Then she turned to Mama. "We'll try it for a few days, but if it doesn't work out, she'll have to go into a lower grade, or the special class." She looked at Rebecca. "Help your cousin learn the routine, but I want no unnecessary talking, and you must speak only in English. Otherwise Ana will never learn."

"I'll take care of her," Rebecca promised as Mama and Aunt Fannie set off for the school's main office. Rebecca was filled with excitement as she showed her cousin where to store her lunch box. Ana was going to be in school with her every day!

Miss Maloney moved one of the students so that the girls could sit side by side at the wooden desks bolted to the floor. She made a quick check to see that the students' hands and faces were clean and their hair neatly combed. The pupils showed her their clean white handkerchiefs. Then Miss Maloney stood at the front of the room.

"Class," she began, and the students sat up straight with their hands folded on their desks. "Since it's Monday morning, and your minds have probably been quite idle during the weekend, we shall begin with some arithmetic teasers. Leo Berg, you are class monitor this week."

Leo walked around importantly and handed out

blank paper at the beginning of each row of desks. When he reached Ana's row, he smirked at her. "Greenie," he said under his breath.

Ana didn't understand what Leo had said and didn't know it was an insult. She gave him a friendly smile. Rebecca fumed. Leo was so nasty!

Ana leaned over and whispered, "What is 'teaser'?"

Rebecca tried to explain quietly. "Miss Maloney gives us numbers to add and subtract. She does it out loud, very fast. We have to do the problem in our heads and then write down the answer." Ana looked puzzled.

Miss Maloney began the exercise, speaking rapidly. "Three plus five, minus two, plus six, minus seven." The students all wrote down their answers, except for Ana. She tapped Rebecca's arm as Miss Maloney launched into the next problem. Rebecca tried to ignore her cousin and concentrate, but by the time Miss Maloney had gotten halfway through the new problem, Rebecca was impossibly lost. She had to leave the answer blank.

"Just add and subtract each number in your head," she explained again. But Ana still didn't understand. Maybe she didn't know the meaning of the words "add" and "subtract," Rebecca thought. There was only one way to make it clear. Covering her mouth and whispering softly, Rebecca began to explain the exercise in Yiddish. She hadn't spoken more than three words when Miss Maloney slapped her ruler against the desk. Rebecca was so startled, she nearly jumped out of her shoes.

"Rebecca Rubin," Miss Maloney said. "Come up here immediately."

Rebecca approached the teacher's large oak desk. "I only needed to give her the directions—"

But Miss Maloney wouldn't listen. "You know the rules," she said. "There is no place in this school for any language except English." She took the dunce cap from a shelf and plopped it on Rebecca's head.

Rebecca walked slowly to the tall stool in the corner of the room, in front of everyone. Her face burned with shame. Leo snickered, and his friends joined in. Soon the entire class was laughing at her. When Rebecca dared to look up, she saw Ana giggling and pointing at the dunce cap.

Her heart sank. Even her cousin was making

"You know the rules," Miss Maloney said.
"There is no place in this school for any language except English."

fun of her! It was the worst punishment Rebecca could imagine. Only Rose looked on with sympathy.

At lunch, Rebecca could barely eat. How could her cousin have laughed at her? When Ana complained about the food Mama had given them, Rebecca was out of patience.

Ana frowned at her bagel. "In Russia we eat bagels when somebody die."

"Bagels aren't just for funerals," Rebecca said curtly. Maybe Ana was afraid it would be bad luck to eat a bagel while Josef was sick at Ellis Island, but Rebecca was too angry to care. "Don't be superstitious," she snapped.

Ana looked confused. She clearly did not understand what Rebecca meant about being superstitious, but she chewed her bagel without another word.

"Greenie! Greenie!" taunted Leo and his friends as they passed by. "Yiddish-talking greenie!"

Rebecca jumped up and yelled back, "Meanie! Meanie! Big fat wienie!" A wienie was a German sausage. That was a good name for Leo, thought Rebecca with satisfaction.

Rose pulled her down. "Ignore them," she said.

28

"You'll only get into more trouble. How many mistakes do you want to make today?"

Rebecca turned her back on the boys. "Even Ana laughed at me," she muttered to Rose, still smarting from the shame. "And I spoke Yiddish to help her!"

"Ana saw the others laughing and thought it must be a joke," Rose explained. "She doesn't know what a dunce cap is."

"What Ana not know?" Rebecca's cousin asked.

"The pointy hat Miss Maloney put on Rebecca is called a dunce cap," Rose told her. "*Dunce* means 'stupid.' It's a punishment for breaking the rules. Rebecca broke the rules by speaking Yiddish in school."

Ana turned pale. "I *not* know!" she protested. "I am sorry, Rebecca. Don't be mad on me."

Rebecca forced a little smile. She didn't want to be angry with her cousin. She wanted to be as close as twins, but now she realized that it wasn't always going to be easy. Even Sadie and Sophie argued sometimes.

"School is difficult," Ana sighed. "My English not so good."

"Don't worry," Rose told her as they finished

eating. "I didn't even know American letters when I first came. Now English is as easy for me as Yiddish. And you're lucky Miss Maloney didn't change your name." She closed her lunch box, and they headed back to their classroom.

"Get different name at school?" Ana asked.

"Oh, sure," Rose said. "Teachers do it all the time. In Russia, my name was Rifka." Ana nodded as if she knew that name. "But on the first day of school, they call me Rose. I was afraid to tell my parents. Then one day the teacher sends home a note. My mother reads it and says, 'Who is this Rose?' When I tell her it's me, she gets so mad!" Rose shrugged. "At home, I'm still Rifka, but here, I am Rose."

Ana shook her head. "I not like to have two names," she said.

As the girls settled down at their desks, Rebecca thought about Aunt Fannie. Was it wrong to give someone an American name? Her aunt had seemed pleased when Rebecca suggested the name Fannie. Her grandfather wanted to be called "Grandpa" instead of the Yiddish word, *Zayda*. And Max had changed his own name from Moyshe. Maybe it was only wrong when it wasn't your choice. How hard it must be to move to another country!

Miss Maloney smoothed her white shirtwaist and clasped her hands primly. "Boys and girls, our class has been chosen to present the morning assembly on Friday. The school has received a new American flag, and we will recite some poems to honor the occasion. Who can tell me how many stars are on the new flag, and why?"

Sarah Goldstein's hand shot into the air. She stood up when Miss Maloney called on her. "In 1912, Arizona and New Mexico became states. Now there are 48 stars on the flag."

"That is correct, Sarah," said the teacher. She pointed to the poetry book she kept on her desk. "Tomorrow I will assign each of you a poem about the flag. You must memorize it by Thursday."

Lucy Valenti raised her hand and asked, "Can we sing a song, too?"

"There's no time for the class to learn a song," Miss Maloney said.

The class groaned with disappointment. "Oh, *please*, Miss Maloney," several students begged.

Miss Maloney thought for a moment. "It might be a good ending to the program. If one of you knows a good patriotic song, I'll consider it," she said. "We'll audition tomorrow, and I'll choose one singer only."

How exciting it would be to sing on the stage, in front of the entire school! All afternoon Rebecca wondered which song she could prepare by tomorrow. Maybe she could learn the song Max had sung when Ana arrived. It was about a flag, and she already knew some of it.

When school ended for the day, several girls crowded together.

"I'm going to sing 'The Star-Spangled Banner,'" Sarah said. "It's all about the flag."

"I'll sing 'Yankee Doodle Dandy,'" Lucy chimed in. "It's not about the flag, but it's very patriotic."

"What means 'patriotic'?" Ana asked.

"That's easy," said Sarah. "It means you love your country and would do anything to defend it."

Ana looked confused. "I love land of Russia," she said, "but I never love tsar, and my brothers won't go in Russian army to fight."

"But now you love America," said Rebecca.

"Maybe someday," Ana said, "if America lets my brother Josef stay. How can Immigration men send him back to Russia just because leg is hurt? Is not right."

Rebecca had to agree. It *wasn't* fair to hold Josef. If he had injured his leg *after* he had landed in New York, no one would think of sending him back to Russia. But Ana was here to stay, and Rebecca hoped she would love her new country. Maybe being part of the assembly would make her feel more American. Rebecca would try to help.

Music
for a Song

The girls all left school together, but
Rebecca kept walking after her friends
turned the corner for home. "I've got some
shopping to do," she announced to Ana.

"You have money for buying?" Ana asked.

Rebecca jingled four pennies in the pocket of her
sweater. She had told Mama she might treat Ana to
a seltzer, but she could do that another day. As long
as Mr. Rossi didn't cause trouble, Ana would be
living with her for a long time, and today Rebecca
needed something important.

"I've got to find the words and music to the
song I want to sing at school," she said. "Just wait
till you see all the pushcarts on Orchard Street. You

can buy anything there. Each peddler sells something different. Pickles, fish, apples, pots and pans, cloth, hats—and music!"

The sun had warmed the air, and the girls strolled arm in arm. "That's Mr. Goldberg's candy shop," Rebecca said, pointing to a store with a striped awning over the front window and displays of candy-covered almonds and fancy chocolates. "He makes the best egg creams and plays the best music."

"What is egg cream?" Ana asked.

Rebecca squeezed her cousin's arm. "Oh, Ana, you're in for a treat. I'll take you when I get my allowance next Saturday. An egg cream is a chocolate-flavored soda. There's no egg in it, or cream," she explained, "but there's milk, and it has a big, bubbly top. It's smooth!"

"Smooth?" Ana repeated.

Rebecca smiled, thinking of how often her older sisters used the word. "*Smooth* means 'modern and wonderful,' all at once!"

"American way of speaking is strange," Ana observed. "Smooth means wonderful, and egg cream has no egg and no cream!" The girls giggled.

They walked until they came closer to the towering tenement buildings that crowded the Lower East Side. Ana stood still. "Is dark here," she said. "Not smooth."

"Don't worry," Rebecca reassured her. But Ana didn't look convinced. Horse-drawn wagons and carts crowded the streets, and horse droppings littered the road, their foul smell rising in the air. Boys in large-brimmed caps pitched bottle tops against a tall stoop. They punched and jostled each other, laughing loudly. The crowds grew thicker, and soon it seemed to Rebecca as if she and Ana were pushing against every person who had ever come to America.

Ana gripped Rebecca's arm as a train clattered by on elevated tracks with a deafening roar.

"People live here?" Ana asked, peering into the dark, open hallway of a tenement building. Smells of boiled cabbage filled the air.

"Bubbie, Grandpa, and Mama lived near here when they first came to America," Rebecca said. "The rent is cheap." She pointed high up at a sooty window behind a fire escape. "Mama and Papa lived right there when they first got married, and even after Sadie, Sophie, and Victor were born." Rebecca was glad they now lived blocks away in their row house, with large windows facing the front and the back. Even on the hottest days, fresh air moved through the apartment. "Don't worry," Rebecca reassured her cousin. "You're not going to live here—just shop."

As they turned onto Orchard Street, the din of many voices rose about them almost as loud as the roar of the train. Peddlers shouted what they had to sell, and shoppers touched, squeezed, argued, bargained, and bought.

"Listen!" Ana shouted. "I hear Yiddish!" Her face lit up with pleasure.

"Sure," Rebecca laughed. "Practically everyone here speaks Yiddish."

So many carts lined the street that there was room for no other traffic than the people who trudged along on foot. Women carried large baskets or oilcloth bags bulging with potatoes, cabbages, and carrots. Knots of men stood and talked, gesturing with their hands.

"What are yellow things?" Ana asked, pointing to a cart piled high.

"Why, those are bananas," Rebecca said. "Haven't you ever eaten one?" Ana shook her head, but Rebecca didn't stop to explain. "There!" she exclaimed, pointing just ahead. "That man is selling sheet music." Rebecca stepped up to the tall cart, peering inside. "I'm looking for 'You're a Grand Old Flag,'" she told the peddler.

"Oy, such a little thing and already buying music," said the peddler, sifting quickly through the piles of colorful sheet music. "I'll bet you're playing the piano. In the tenements, they got practically nothing to eat, but a piano they got!"

Rebecca shook her head. "My teacher will play the piano. I'm going to sing in a school assembly." At least she hoped she was. Right now, she needed the words to the song to even have a chance.

The peddler pulled a red, white, and blue cover from deep under the jumbled pile. "The great music of George M. Cohan!" he bellowed. "*Mazel tov!* Congratulations! Today is your lucky day. A special price I'm giving on sheet music. So today you'll take this almost new copy for only ten cents."

"Ten cents?" Rebecca gulped. But she knew you never paid the asking price for anything on Orchard Street. She tried to remember how Bubbie got the peddlers to lower their prices. Bubbie argued and sometimes even insulted them, although nobody seemed to take it seriously.

"A robber!" Rebecca yelled. "A robber trying to trick a little girl!"

"*Shah!*" scolded the peddler. "You want to scare away all my customers?" He waved the sheet music just out of her reach. "Look at how perfect. Every page is here, and there isn't so much as a crease on the cover. So, I'll make you a bargain like you never heard. Take it home for just seven cents!"

"You think I'm a millionaire?" Rebecca asked, stalling for time. How could she get the man to lower the price again?

Ana's eyes were wide. "How much money do you have?" she whispered.

"Not that much!" Rebecca whispered back.

But the peddler heard every word, as if his hearing was tuned to the sound of every pigeon feather that dropped onto the sidewalk. "For such

"You think I'm a millionaire?" Rebecca asked, stalling for time.
How could she get the man to lower the price again?

a talented singer, I'll give it away practically free for a nickel!"

Rebecca looked at the music. Here were the words she needed and the notes Miss Maloney could play on the piano in the assembly hall, if only she chose Rebecca to sing! She fingered the pennies in her pocket.

"There's a tear on the back cover," she said. "Two cents."

"You want my children should starve in the street?" yelled the peddler. He put his hand over his heart, as if it were breaking.

If the peddler was going to be dramatic, Rebecca decided that might work for her, too. She pulled out her handkerchief and sniffled into it. "I can only spend three pennies," she whimpered, handing the music back. "Here, mister. I don't have to sing at the assembly." She looked up with sad eyes and started to leave. Ana patted her shoulder sympathetically, but as they walked away, Rebecca winked at her.

"Such children!" the peddler cried. "Like my own little girls. So you'll take it for three cents! This week I won't eat."

Rebecca beamed. She quickly handed over the

pennies and took the sheet music. Then she steered Ana back to the banana peddler.

"I have here a young lady who has never eaten a banana," she said. "How many for one penny?" The man handed Rebecca two ripe bananas.

Ana spoke up. "That's all?" she asked, sounding insulted. "Only two for a whole penny?"

Rebecca stared in amazement. Her cousin really did catch on quickly.

The man handed her two green bananas. "Two for now, two for tomorrow," he said.

Rebecca paid her penny. She handed a ripe banana to her cousin, who promptly bit into the skin.

"No, no!" Rebecca cried. "Don't eat that." She peeled her banana to expose the fruit, and Ana did the same. "Now try it," Rebecca said.

Ana took a big bite. "Is wonderful," she said. "Fruit with its own wrapping! And I get four bananas for price of two."

Rebecca grinned. "That's what I call bargaining! Don't ever pay what they ask," she advised. "It's the first rule of living in New York."

"We play game with peddlers," Ana laughed. "We are smooth!"

TWO SONGBIRDS

Rebecca had barely slept at all Monday night, going over the words to the song in her head. She didn't want to forget them in the middle of the audition! Tuesday morning she dressed quickly, eager to get to school. She tucked her doll into her pocket. "Wish me luck," she whispered to the wooden Beckie doll.

The morning routine was as hectic as it had been the day before. First Rebecca had to wait her turn to use the toilet in the hallway, then wait for a chance to wash at the sink, and finally wait for a chair to sit down for breakfast.

Papa and Uncle Jacob talked rapidly in Yiddish. "I went to all the builders, and none of them wanted a cabinet maker. No one wants to hire a new immigrant," Uncle Jacob said. "One man told me to try the garment factories." He shrugged. "I suppose if I can cut a board, I can cut a piece of cloth."

"You don't want to work in a sweatshop," said Papa. "It's not healthy, and the pay is terrible." His forehead creased into a frown. "I wish the shoe store had more business. Then you could work with me."

"I know," Uncle Jacob said. "But you've done enough, Louis. I'm willing to take any job for a start."

As the girls headed off to school, Rebecca stopped in the entry to tuck the sheet music safely inside her coat. Pasta appeared from nowhere and rubbed against Rebecca's leg. She bent down to stroke the cat's fur, but it slipped out of reach and padded down to the basement. Outside, a cold drizzle fell, and the girls stepped up the pace.

"Today my papa is looking again for job," Ana said. "And your papa is going to Hebrew Immigrant Aid Society." Ana's face was pale. "I am afraid for my brother if infection on leg doesn't go away."

Rebecca couldn't think of anything to say. Ana was right—it made no sense that an injured leg could keep a boy out of the country. Besides, if

Josef was too sick to stay in America, how could he go back to Russia alone?

Rebecca tried to take her mind off Josef by thinking about the audition. If just one of her classmates sang better than she did, Rebecca wouldn't be chosen to sing in the assembly.

As soon as the class had recited the Pledge of Allegiance, the students sat with their hands folded on their desks.

"We're going to start right off with the audition," Miss Maloney said. "We have very little time to prepare for this assembly, and I want it to go perfectly." She looked around the room. "Who would like to try a song?"

Five students raised their hands, including Rebecca. Two boys started off, and each one sang in a high, clear voice. But their songs had nothing to do with the flag or America. Rebecca was next.

Leo hid behind a book and stuck out his tongue at her. Rebecca turned her eyes away. She wasn't going to let Leo ruin her audition. She reached into her pocket and patted Beckie for luck. Then she sang out with a big smile. She imitated Max, giving the song rhythm. The other students began to clap along with her singing. Rebecca held her head high and marched in place. When she got to the last words of the song—"Keep your eye on the grand old flag!"—she gave a sharp salute.

But Miss Maloney only said, "Thank you, Rebecca." Next, Sarah sailed through "The Star-Spangled Banner," but her ending was off-key. Finally, Lucy sang "Yankee Doodle Dandy." Rebecca's heart beat faster as Miss Maloney made her decision.

"I think you've all voted with your clapping," she said at last. "While each of our singers did well, I like the enthusiasm you showed for Rebecca's lively song. It seems just right for the assembly. It will be our grand finale!" Miss Maloney picked up a stack of papers. "Now I'll pass out some poems for you to learn. Since there are forty-two students in our class, each poem will be recited by two students together."

Rebecca squeezed her doll through her pocket and thought, *I'm going to sing for the entire school!* She pictured herself standing on the stage, singing along with the gay notes of the piano. She could almost hear the applause.

"Pay attention, Rebecca!" Miss Maloney was

standing in front of her. Rebecca blinked as Miss Maloney repeated her words. "These poems are too hard for Ana, and I can't take a chance on anyone making mistakes at the assembly. Instead, I've decided to have her sing with you. I'm trusting you to teach her the song at home."

Rebecca was speechless. She had worked so hard for the chance to sing a solo, and now she would have to share it with her cousin. Immediately, she felt ashamed of her selfish thoughts.

Beside her, Ana opened the sheet music. "You're grend old fleg," she murmured.

Why, Ana can barely pronounce the words! thought Rebecca with alarm. Miss Maloney had said she couldn't take a chance on anyone making a mistake. What if Ana did? It would be so embarrassing!

Miss Maloney turned to write on the blackboard, and Lucy passed Rebecca a crumpled note. As Rebecca unfolded it, she glanced up. Lucy looked as if she was about to cry.

"No fair!" the note said. "Ana doesn't even know the song. She shouldn't get to sing."

Lucy must feel terrible, thought Rebecca. Lucy had auditioned, yet she wouldn't get to sing at all.

Rebecca felt sorry for her friend, and she hoped Lucy wasn't blaming her. She stuffed the note into her pocket before Miss Maloney caught her.

Rebecca couldn't keep her mind on her work, and she was grateful when Miss Maloney took the class up on the roof for some exercise. The rain had stopped, and pale sunlight pushed through the clouds. Rose and several other girls surrounded Rebecca and Ana.

"You're so lucky," Rose said to Ana. "You've only been in school for two days, and now you're going to sing at the assembly!"

Ana clasped her hands together nervously. "I hope I can learn fastly," she said. She turned and smiled warmly at Rebecca. "But I not worry. My cousin will teach me."

Ana went off to try jumping rope with some of the girls, but Rebecca headed over to Lucy and Sarah. "I didn't ask Miss Maloney to let Ana sing," Rebecca explained. "It's not my fault."

"It's still not fair," Lucy said firmly. "She can barely speak English. How can she learn the song?"

"If she ruins the performance, the whole school will be laughing at us," Sarah added. "You're going to have to do a good job teaching her the song, or it *will* be your fault."

Rebecca's stomach tightened into a knot.

Rebecca was quiet on the way home, while Ana bubbled over with excitement. As they headed up the front stoop, Rebecca saw Mr. Rossi's curtains flap closed. Was he spying to see if Ana and her family had moved yet?

Ana raced up the steps, and in a stream of Yiddish, happily told Aunt Fannie and Mama about the assembly.

"*Mazel tov!* Congratulations!" said Aunt Fannie. She hugged Ana. "I'm so glad you are happy in the American school."

"We'd better practice," Rebecca said, "if you're going to learn the song." She took two apples from the bowl on the table. "Come on, Ana, I'll take you to the best place in the building." Ana followed Rebecca up the hall stairs, past Bubbie and Grandpa's apartment, all the way to the top of the stairway. Rebecca pushed open a rickety wooden door, and the girls stepped out onto the flat rooftop. There was a soft ruffling of feathers, and cooing sounds.

"Birds!" Ana exclaimed, rushing to the wire cages stacked along one side of the roof.

"They're pigeons," Rebecca said. "They belong to Mr. Rossi, but I like to come up and look at them. I think they know me." She bit off a piece of her apple and held it up to a cage. A tan bird with black spots on its wings eagerly pecked at it. Rebecca reached in two fingers and gently stroked its feathers.

"It's hard to imagine grouchy Mr. Rossi keeping birds, isn't it," Rebecca said as the girls fed them pieces of apple.

Ana nodded. When her apple was gone, she took the sheet music from Rebecca. "I'm so glad we will sing together at assembly," Ana said. "We will be two songbirds." She began to sing.

Rebecca listened as her cousin's melodic notes rose above the cooing of the pigeons. At least Ana had a pretty voice. If she could learn to pronounce the words properly, she might make a good singing partner. If not, the performance would be ruined.

Carefully, Rebecca had her cousin repeat the words. "It's not 'grend,'" she explained patiently, "but 'grand.' Listen to the a-a-a sound." Ana

repeated the word until she got it right. Then they went on to the word "flag," and the same problem came back.

"No, no, no," Rebecca said, feeling exasperated. "It's fl-a-a-a-g, not fl-eh-g." But Ana couldn't seem to remember from one verse to the next. Over and over again, they sang the verses, but Ana either forgot the words or mispronounced them.

If Ana can't sing the song properly, Rebecca thought, *I'll be humiliated. And what's worse, my class will be embarrassed before the entire school.*

The wooden door creaked open, and Victor

51

and Michael stepped out onto the roof.

"Beckie, Mama wants you girls to set the table," Victor said. "She's determined to get all thirteen of us in the parlor for dinner. Grandpa's bringing down more chairs."

"What have you heard about Josef?" Ana asked her brother, speaking in Yiddish.

Michael's slender body slouched against the wall. His short hair seemed as stiff as bristles on a new brush. "Josef is still sick with a fever from his infected leg. Doctors are treating him at the Ellis Island infirmary, but they don't know if his leg will heal." Michael touched Ana's shoulder, and Rebecca saw that his hand was shaking. "If Josef loses his leg, he will have to go back to Russia."

"That would be so unfair," Rebecca said angrily. "Why does it matter if someone has an injured leg?"

"Papa told me that every immigrant has to be able to support himself," Victor explained. "A lame person can't work."

"That's ridiculous," Rebecca exclaimed. "Josef is only fifteen. His family will take care of him. Even if he is lame, he could be a lawyer or a bank clerk who sits at a desk all day!"

Victor shrugged. "Papa says it's the law."

"Well, it's a bad law," Rebecca declared.

Michael spoke up. "There's some good news, too. Papa found a job today, cutting cloth for coats."

Rebecca couldn't stop herself. "He's going to work in a sweatshop?" she blurted out.

Michael shrugged. "It's only until a better job comes along." He stood a little straighter. "I'm going to work, too. The dairy company needs boys to move the big milk cans from the delivery wagons to the warehouse. Papa told the manager I was fourteen." He flexed his skinny arm. "The cans might be a bit heavy, but I will build up my muscles."

"What about school?" Rebecca asked.

"Since Josef isn't here, I must help earn money," Michael said. Then he looked a bit doubtful. "Maybe I can go to school at night—if I'm not too tired."

Why are things going so wrong? Rebecca asked herself. If Josef were sent back to Russia, his family would never see him again. Uncle Jacob had taken a job in a factory, where he would work long hours under terrible conditions. And now Michael had to leave school.

The rooftop door opened, and Mr. Rossi stood glaring at them. He held a pail of birdseed.

"This roof is not a playground. *Shoo!*" he called, as if they were birds who could fly away. Then Mr. Rossi realized exactly who was on the roof.

"You still here?" he asked Michael. "You can't stay any longer. I am telling landlord tomorrow."

"You don't need to tell the landlord anything, Mr. Rossi," Victor said. "My uncle just rented a tenement on Orchard Street. The whole family is going to move next week."

Fear filled Ana's eyes. "Orchard Street?" she echoed. "The place with dark buildings and big noises and—" Her voice broke as she turned to Rebecca. "I don't want to leave," she cried. "You are like sister to me." Rebecca reached out to hug her cousin, but Ana ran from the rooftop, leaving Rebecca and the cooing birds behind her.

"Now," Mr. Rossi said, "the rest of you, off the roof!"

CHAPTER
FIVE
—

A NEW FLAG
WAVES

That night, Rebecca tried to comfort her cousin, but Ana's tears wouldn't stop. She cried herself to sleep, her handkerchief still clutched in her hand.

Rebecca tossed and turned, thinking about Ana moving to Orchard Street. Next week, Ana would go to a different school. Rebecca had expected her cousin to live with her for a long time and be her partner in everything. She remembered the excitement of bargaining with the peddlers, and thought about how much fun it was to dress alike. Just as Ana had said, they were like sisters. Even better—they were like twins.

It was wonderful having Ana with her all the

time—at least, it was wonderful until Miss Maloney decided Ana should sing in the assembly. Now Rebecca's stomach twisted into knots whenever she thought about the performance. This was one thing she didn't want to do with Ana.

By morning, Rebecca was too tired to even talk, but it hardly mattered. Ana barely said a word all the way to school. Her eyes were puffy, and she seemed ready to cry again at any moment. Rebecca was silent, too, as the class filed into the big auditorium for rehearsal. The students lined up on the stage, facing the empty chairs where the rest of the school would sit in just two days.

"You may read your poems today, since it's just the first practice," Miss Maloney said. "But tomorrow is already Thursday, and you must have them memorized by then. Remember that this assembly is to show our respect for the flag. I expect each of you to recite your poems perfectly and with great feeling. Leo," Miss Maloney called, "you will begin the program by explaining why we have a new flag. Step forward, please."

Leo straightened his tweed jacket and puffed

out his chest. "In 1912, America welcomed two new states to the Union," he began.

When Leo finished introducing the program, Lucy Valenti and Gertie Lowenstein read their poem.

"'Flag Song,' by Lydia Avery Coonley Ward," the girls said in unison.

> *"Out on the breeze, o'er land and seas,*
> *A beautiful banner is streaming.*
> *Shining its stars, splendid its bars,*
> *Under the sunshine 'tis gleaming."*

When they finished the last lines, two boys stepped forward. "'America for Me,' by Henry van Dyke," they announced.

All through the rehearsal Rebecca fidgeted, anxiously awaiting her moment on the stage. She knew the song perfectly now. If only Ana would sing without any mistakes!

When all the other students had recited their pieces, Rebecca and Ana moved to the front of the stage. Miss Maloney sat down at the piano, spreading her silky black skirt across the piano stool. She opened the sheet music and played the opening notes. The girls began to sing.

Ana's rich voice sounded even prettier with the piano to accompany her. Rebecca tried to close her ears to her cousin's accent. Although Rebecca had drilled her repeatedly, Ana just couldn't seem to pronounce a short "a" sound. She said "fleg" instead of "flag" and "lend" instead of "land." As Rebecca boomed out the last two lines, she suddenly realized she was singing alone. Ana had forgotten the words completely! Ana looked at her in panic and then ran from the stage, her footsteps echoing down the hallway. Rebecca stood alone, her voice trailing off. Her classmates groaned.

"Let's be polite, children," Miss Maloney scolded them. "Rebecca and Ana are still learning the song."

Me? thought Rebecca. *Why, I know the song perfectly. It's Ana who's spoiling it!*

When the rehearsal was over, Rebecca found Ana alone in the classroom. As the other students filed in, Ana murmured, "I practice harder." She looked up at Rebecca. "You will help?"

Rebecca couldn't even answer. She took her pencil to the pencil sharpener, feeling the other students' eyes on her as she walked across the room.

Sarah cornered her. "Ana barely knows the words, and when she does, she can't say them in proper English."

"Shhh," Rebecca said. "She might hear you." She turned the pencil sharpener handle harder until the lead point was as sharp as a needle. "What can I do?" she demanded in a loud whisper. "*I'm* not the one making the mistakes!"

"Well, she's *your* cousin," Sarah said. She twisted a fold of her dress anxiously. "Please don't let her ruin the assembly. Our class will be the laughingstock of the school!" She put her hand on Rebecca's shoulder. "Why don't you just tell her she can't sing with you?"

Gertie chimed in from her seat nearby. "That would solve the whole problem. I'm sure Miss Maloney would agree. She said everything has to be perfect to show our respect for the flag."

Rebecca walked slowly back to her desk. Everyone was counting on her. *It will be my fault if the assembly is ruined,* she thought. Should she tell her cousin not to sing?

Then Rebecca thought of something else. Perhaps

Ana didn't *want* to sing anymore. Now that she saw how difficult it was, she might be relieved if she didn't have to practice the words and worry about saying them perfectly. Next week, she would be going to a different school anyway, so maybe being part of the assembly didn't matter to her now.

When the class was dismissed for lunch, Ana stayed at her desk, hunched over the sheet music. Rebecca dawdled at the closet when she got her lunch box. *Maybe this is the time to tell Ana not to sing,* she thought. Then she heard her cousin's voice floating softly across the room. "You're grend old fleg and high-flyink fleg . . ." Rebecca grabbed her lunch box and hurried out to find Rose.

"Where's *Enna?*" Otto Geller teased as Rebecca rushed by. "Is she looking at the *fleg?*"

Rebecca's face flushed with anger. She turned her back on Otto and marched over to join Rose.

"Everyone thinks it will be my fault if Ana ruins the assembly," Rebecca said to Rose as she sat down beside her.

Rose unwrapped a knish and took a bite of the potato-filled pastry. "What do *you* think?" she asked.

knish

"I've tried to teach her the song, but there isn't enough time," Rebecca replied. "I think Ana might make a lot of mistakes."

"She might," Rose agreed. "It's hard to learn English, and Ana's only been here a few days."

"If the assembly is ruined because of Ana, the whole class will be disappointed, including Miss Maloney. And I'll be the one who let them down. I bet no one will ever speak to me again."

Rose looked doubtful. "How long do you really think they'll remember?"

"Probably forever," said Rebecca. She still remembered her humiliation when Miss Maloney made her wear the dunce cap. But Rebecca suddenly realized that she hadn't thought about the dunce cap at all since that day. And none of her classmates had said a word about the dunce cap, not even Leo.

Rebecca nibbled at her lunch. "Sarah thinks I should tell Ana she can't sing with me. Maybe she's right. I'm sure Ana's worried about spoiling the song," Rebecca pointed out. "She must be worried, or she wouldn't have run off the stage this morning when she forgot the words. She might be relieved if I tell her not to sing."

"Maybe." Rose shrugged. "How would *you* feel if you were Ana?"

"Well, I know I wouldn't want to be embarrassed in front of the whole school," said Rebecca.

Miss Maloney rang the bell, and Rebecca followed Rose back to class. She had eaten only a few bites, but she didn't feel hungry at all.

Rose's question burned in her head for the rest of the day. *How would you feel?* Rebecca already knew how she'd feel if Ana *did* sing and made mistakes. But how would Ana feel if Rebecca kept her out of the assembly?

As soon as she opened her eyes Friday morning, Rebecca felt knots in the pit of her stomach. The rehearsal had gone no better the day before. Ana either forgot the words or pronounced them wrong. Miss Maloney had looked at the girls with pursed lips and hadn't said a word. Rebecca couldn't bear to let everyone down, especially her teacher.

Now the assembly was starting in just a few hours. If she was going to tell Ana not to sing, she had to do it soon. But Ana had already gone into the kitchen for breakfast. Quickly, Rebecca began getting dressed.

Rose's question pricked at her. *How would you feel if you were Ana?*

Well, how *would* she feel? Rebecca looked in the mirror and pictured Ana saying to her, "Your voice not so pretty. I not want you to sing with me." Abruptly, Rebecca sat down hard on the bed as a hot wave of terrible feelings washed over her. She blinked, and then again she imagined it, Ana telling her not to sing. Again her chest burned with hurt and humiliation. The feeling was far, far worse than the embarrassment she had felt onstage when Ana forgot the words. Rebecca swallowed. Her mouth felt dry. She knew she would never forget it if Ana were to push her out of the assembly.

Mama beamed at the girls over breakfast. "It's so nice to see you matching every day." Rebecca managed a thin smile, but Ana didn't even look up.

Aunt Fannie handed each girl a small American flag. "We got these at Immigration when we came," she said. "Maybe they will bring you luck this morning when you sing."

Rebecca thanked her aunt politely and gave her

flag a limp wave. Ana simply dropped hers into her pocket.

Bubbie came in with a plate of dark rolls, and Grandpa poked his head in the door. "I'll handle the store myself this morning," he said to Papa. "I hope everything goes well with Josef."

Papa, Aunt Fannie, and Uncle Jacob were going to Ellis Island once again. Josef's fever had broken, and the Hebrew Immigrant Aid Society had arranged for the family to meet with immigration officials. Rebecca's aunt had replaced her kerchief with one of Mama's hats, and Uncle Jacob had trimmed his beard neatly.

Suddenly Aunt Fannie sank into a chair. "What if the immigration men say Josef cannot stay?" she worried. "I could never forgive them."

It would be wrong to force Josef to leave America just because his leg wasn't perfect, Rebecca felt certain. Now she realized it would also be wrong to force Ana out of the assembly just because her English wasn't perfect. Maybe Rebecca and her classmates would be embarrassed if the song was a flop, but in just a few days, nobody would remember or care. Yet if she told Ana not to sing . . .

Rebecca ran to the bedroom and grabbed her doll from the pillow. *Please bring good luck today,* she whispered and slipped Beckie into her pocket.

As the girls headed down the street to school, Ana looked directly at Rebecca. "Don't worry," she said. "I not sing today and ruin assembly."

Rebecca stopped still. "What do you mean? I didn't say anything about your singing." A shiver of shame crept up her neck. How could Ana have known what she had been thinking?

"You don't have to say anything to me," Ana said softly. "I hear you and Sarah and Lucy talking. You think I am dunce?"

Rebecca's heart sank. "I *was* worried about the performance," she admitted, "but now—now I *do* want you to sing with me, Ana. Honest."

"Now is too late," Ana said. "I tried hard, but I know things not always fair. Just like with Josef." She rushed ahead, leaving Rebecca to walk the rest of the way alone.

At school, Rebecca tried to talk to Ana as they filed into the auditorium. "We're two songbirds— remember?" But Ana turned away.

The class crowded together near the stage steps

as Miss Maloney went to turn on the stage lights. Sarah pulled Rebecca aside.

"Did you tell her?" she whispered. Rebecca shook her head. Sarah didn't make a sound, but her mouth moved to form the words "Oh, no!"

Rebecca turned away, fighting back tears. Now *everyone* was unhappy with her. The performance hadn't even begun, and already she had ruined everything.

"Are we ready?" Miss Maloney said cheerily. "Line up, boys and girls."

As the students formed a line, Rebecca gazed at the high ceiling and the dark paneled walls. In gold lettering along the top of the walls were the names of famous Americans: George Washington, Thomas Jefferson, Abraham Lincoln. She felt as if they were ready to welcome the new flag, too. But was she?

Rebecca took a deep breath and walked over to Ana. Her cousin had not joined the line of classmates waiting to step onto the stage. Rebecca pulled her Russian doll from her pocket. "You take Beckie," she said, handing the doll to Ana. "She brought me good luck in the audition, and now she'll bring us both good luck in the assembly."

Ana held the little doll close. "Do you really think I should sing, Rebecca?" she asked softly.

"Of course you should," Rebecca assured her. "You have the prettiest voice in the class. Now come on, let's get in line!"

Feet shuffled and chairs creaked while the audience filed in to their seats. Then silence fell as Miss Maloney stepped to the front of the stage and welcomed the school to the assembly.

Leo began his opening speech, but Rebecca's heart was beating so loudly, she barely heard him. She looked out at the sea of upturned faces and drew in a shaky breath. There were so many people, all listening in complete silence. Would they notice every mistake? As her classmates recited their poems, Rebecca's hands began to tremble. It was almost time for her and Ana to sing.

At last, Miss Maloney played the lively opening notes on the piano, and the girls stepped forward. Together, they began the bouncy tune. Rebecca tried to smile and concentrate on her own singing. She barely noticed her cousin's accent and hoped the audience didn't notice it, either. Ana's strong voice lifted Rebecca's, and Rebecca's clear words carried

Rebecca tried to smile and concentrate on her own singing. She barely noticed her cousin's accent and hoped the audience didn't notice it, either.

Ana's. When they came to the last verse, Rebecca realized that the audience was clapping in rhythm and the assembly seemed alive with enthusiasm. They had nearly made it to the end.

As the piano sounded its final chord, Ana suddenly pulled the small American flag from her pocket and waved it high. Surprised, Rebecca quickly did the same. The entire school cheered and applauded.

Then the lights dimmed, and a bright light shone on the new flag that hung from a pole at the side of the stage. Its rich colors stood out in the darkened hall. The audience rose, and everyone placed their right hands over their hearts and recited the Pledge of Allegiance. But Rebecca's ears were still ringing with the sound of applause. She and Ana had done it. They had sung for the whole school, and everything had been all right. Ana's accent hadn't mattered at all. And now Miss Maloney was beaming proudly as the principal came onstage and shook her hand. The assembly was a success.

Rebecca thought she saw tears brimming in Ana's eyes, but her cousin's face was lit up with happiness. Rebecca squeezed Ana's hand, and Ana squeezed back.

"Why did you wave your flag?" Rebecca whispered.

"I am feeling *patriotic*," Ana said, motioning to the back of the audience. "Look!"

Rebecca peered through the dim light and saw a row of people standing near the wall. She could see her mother, her father, Uncle Jacob, and Aunt Fannie—and beside them was a tall, lanky boy with a thickly bandaged leg, leaning on a wooden crutch. Rebecca waved her flag in his direction, and from his pocket, Josef pulled an identical flag and waved it high in the air.

LOOKING BACK

SCHOOL
IN
1914

When immigrant families like Ana's came to America, they were grateful for the chance to send their children to school. Most of the countries the immigrants had lived in before didn't have free schools, so poor children couldn't attend. In Russia, schools had quotas that allowed only a very few Jewish children. Parents like Jacob and Fannie knew that with an education, their children would get better jobs and have easier lives. Jewish parents valued education and felt that one of the best things about America was the free schools. They held teachers in high regard and encouraged their children to excel in school.

At first, immigrant children were usually placed in special classes for students who didn't know English. Within four or five months, they would move into regular

Schoolchildren having a hygiene inspection

classes, though often below the grade for their age, especially if they'd never been to school before.

In big city schools, the first order of the day was the *hygiene*, or cleanliness, inspection. The students held out their hands to show that they were clean. The teacher also examined faces, ears, necks, and scalps. With as many as 50 or more children crowded into a classroom, sickness spread quickly, so keeping clean was important. If the hygiene inspection revealed a dirty neck or face, the student would be sent to the restroom to wash up.

Sometimes, tiny insects called *lice* infested children's hair. Students with lice were sent home, where their

To get rid of lice, some people shampooed with vinegar or kerosene.

Many families had no bathroom at home. Once a week, tenement children might bathe at a public bathhouse, like this one.

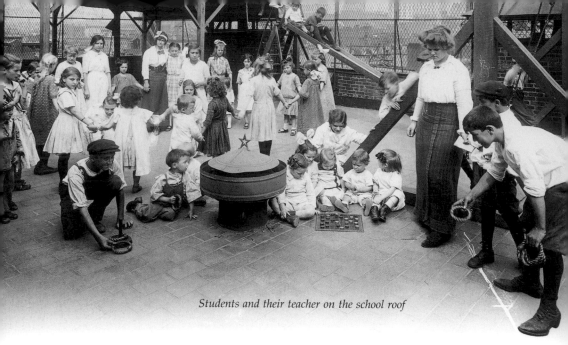

Students and their teacher on the school roof

mothers had to wash their hair with strong soap and boil their clothes and sheets to kill the lice.

Rebecca's school day was different from school today in other ways, too. There was no playground, no gym, and no recess. Instead, the students did stretching and breathing exercises right at their desks. Occasionally, the teacher would take the students outdoors for some fresh air and physical exercise. In big city schools, often the only space outdoors was on the roof!

At school, children were expected to be quiet and orderly. To keep 50 or more children quiet and orderly for six or seven hours was no easy task, so teachers were often quite strict. Some teachers punished students who broke rules or failed their lessons by hitting them with a cane or ruler. Others relied on shaming the students by scolding them in front of the class or making them wear

*A schoolgirl
wearing a
dunce cap*

a dunce cap, as Miss Maloney did. Still, most girls liked and admired their teachers. One woman said of her childhood teachers, "I loved the way they dressed and the way they spoke. I wanted to be just like them."

Indeed, immigrant families viewed teachers as "models of Americanhood." In cities with lots of immigrants, like New York, the teachers' job was not just to educate the children but to turn them into Americans. The people who ran the schools believed that good Americans were clean, quiet, and orderly--and spoke English. Speaking the language of your old country was considered shameful. One Jewish woman remembered

A nursery school for immigrant children taught its young students to be patriotic.

This girl works at a box factory, and the boy is selling newspapers.

that when she was a girl, "I was embarrassed to speak Yiddish to my mother. . . . You tried to talk English all the time. We were very anxious to become American."

By law, children were supposed to stay in school until age 14, but many families sent younger children to work because the families desperately needed the money. Jobs for children included selling newspapers, shining shoes, delivering packages, and working in factories. Girls were often kept out of school to care for their younger siblings while their parents worked. And studying at home was nearly impossible in the cramped, dark, noisy buildings the immigrants lived in.

Rebecca's part of New York City, now called the Lower East Side, had once been a neighborhood of *row houses*—three- or four-story homes meant for a single family. But as thousands of immigrants began moving in, landlords divided the row houses into *flats*, with one or more families on each floor. Rebecca's row house was divided this way. Still, her apartment was a little larger and nicer than the *tenements* in the

Row houses

Tenements were so cramped that children often played out on the street.

more crowded parts of the Lower East Side. Tenements were cold and damp in the winter, hot and stuffy in the summer, and dark and smelly all the time. No wonder Ana was worried about moving into one!

Over the years, the immigrants gradually got better jobs and found better housing, just as Rebecca's parents did. As their children grew up and started families of their own, many of them left the Lower East Side and moved to other parts of New York—or to other cities and states—to raise their own families. By the time immigrants like Ana and Rose were grown up, they felt completely at home in America. But they never forgot the teachers who had first helped them to become Americans.

This New Year's Day card shows a happy Jewish American family in the 1940s— when Rebecca and Ana would have been raising families of their own.

GLOSSARY

Amerikanka *(ah-mair-ee-KONG-kah)*—the Russian way to
say **American**

bubbie *(BUH-bee)*—**grandmother** in Yiddish

knish *(kuh-NISH)*—in Yiddish, a food made of **dough stuffed
with a filling,** such as potato, then baked or fried

mazel tov *(MAH-zl tof)*—Hebrew for **congratulations!**

rugalach *(ROO-gul-ahk)*—a Yiddish word meaning "little
twists"; a small **pastry,** often filled with nuts or jam

samovar *(SAM-oh-var)*—a tall **Russian urn** used to heat water
for tea

scusi *(SKOO-zee)*—**Excuse me** in Italian

schlepping *(SHLEP-ing)*—a Yiddish word that means
hauling or **lugging**

shah *(shah)*—the Yiddish way to say **shush!**

tsar *(zar; often spelled "czar")*—the Russian word for **emperor**

zayda *(ZAY-dah)*—**grandfather** in Yiddish

A SNEAK PEEK AT

CANDLELIGHT FOR

When Miss Maloney assigns a Christmas project,
Rebecca isn't sure what to do. She wants to please her
teacher—but what will her family think?

Rebecca Rubin and her friend Rose Krensky pushed against a biting wind as they made their way to school. Most of the shops were still closed, and the streets were quieter than usual.

"I'm freezing," Rebecca said.

"I have goosebumples," Rose complained.

Rebecca giggled. "You mixed up two words, but I like it. I have goosebumples, too."

The air held a hint of snow, and Rebecca felt a shiver of excitement. Winter weather meant it was almost time for Hanukkah, her favorite holiday.

All around, Rebecca saw Christmas decorations. "It seems like everything is red and green," she said to Rose. Store windows were framed in pine boughs, and some displayed miniature trees decorated with shiny glass balls and glittering ropes of tinsel. The doors on many of the row houses had pine wreaths with bright red ribbons. It seemed as if the entire neighborhood had changed from its drab everyday clothes into its best holiday outfit.

"I love seeing the candles in our menorah," Rebecca said, "but there really aren't any special decorations for Hanukkah, are there?"

"I love seeing the candles in our menorah," Rebecca said, "but there really aren't any special decorations for Hanukkah, are there?"

81

"Sure there are," Rose replied with a sly smile. "We decorate our plates with *latkes,* and then we eat them!"

Rebecca could almost smell the crisply fried potato pancakes. "My mother's been buying potatoes by the bagful," she said. "We're going to make tons of latkes. My cousin Ana and her family are coming over on Friday night to celebrate the first night of Hanukkah. I can hardly wait!"

latkes

When they arrived at the schoolyard, Rebecca and Rose hopped up and down, trying to stay warm. As soon as Miss Maloney rang her big brass bell, they hurried into the classroom. The radiators hissed, but the room was so cold that Rebecca hated to take off her coat and wool scarf. She rubbed her hands together briskly before she folded them on the desk in front of her.

"Let's warm up a bit," Miss Maloney said. "Stand up, everyone." She led the students as they stretched beside their desks, reaching high toward the ceiling. "Inhale," Miss Maloney said. As they bent over to touch their toes, she directed, "Exhale!

Let's get our blood circulating." The room began to warm up, and a thin layer of moisture fogged the windows. The children took deep breaths in and out and moved their arms in little circles, but when Rebecca sat down again, her feet were still freezing.

Miss Maloney placed a wooden crate on her desk. "Since it's almost Christmas," she said, "we are going to make a lovely gift for you to take home to your families." From the box she pulled a bright table decoration. A tall red candle rose from a base of greenery and berries. The fresh scent of pine wafted through the air.

"*Oooh!*" the students exclaimed in admiration.

"I made this centerpiece to show you what yours will look like," Miss Maloney explained. "I have collected all the materials we need." She pointed to the boughs that seemed to sprout from the base of the decoration. "The city allowed me to gather these fresh branches of balsam and pine in Central Park. The berries came from wild rose bushes." Clusters of dried red berries were nestled in the greenery, along with small pinecones. A vivid red bow added a cheerful finishing touch.

Rebecca gulped. They were going to make Christmas decorations! She glanced over at Rose, who wrinkled her forehead doubtfully.

"It's beautiful," sighed Lucy Valenti.

Rose raised her hand and stood stiffly by her desk when Miss Maloney called on her. "Excuse me," Rose said, "but at our house, we don't celebrate Christmas."

Miss Maloney smiled kindly, as if Rose simply didn't understand. "Christmas is a national holiday, children, celebrated by Americans all over the country. At the Capitol in Washington, D.C., there's even a decorated Christmas tree for everyone to enjoy."

Rose opened her mouth as if to argue, but then clamped it shut and sat down without another word.

The teacher set out round wooden disks to use as bases, along with pots of glue and pairs of scissors. She pulled baskets of green boughs from behind her desk and set out an assortment of pine-cones, berries, and rolls of wide ribbon. She carefully unrolled a paper packet filled with candles.

Rebecca wondered if it was true that the entire country celebrated Christmas. Her family didn't. She looked around the room. Her friend Gertie Lowenstein was Jewish, and she was busily gathering greenery for her centerpiece. In fact, everyone in the class buzzed excitedly, except for Rose and Rebecca.

Miss Maloney handed Rebecca a wooden base and a red candle, and Rebecca took them reluctantly. Would it be wrong to do this school project? She hesitated for a moment. Then she selected several full branches to use around the base. The greenery smelled wonderful, almost spicy.

She glanced over at Rose, who looked up and shrugged her shoulders, as if to say, *What can we do?*

Read All of Rebecca's Stories,
available at bookstores and *americangirl.com*.

Meet Rebecca
When Rebecca finds a way to earn money,
she keeps it a secret from her family.

Rebecca and Ana
Rebecca is going to sing for the whole school.
Will cousin Ana ruin her big moment?

Candlelight for Rebecca
Rebecca's family is Jewish.
Is it wrong for Rebecca to make a
Christmas decoration in school?

Rebecca and the Movies
At the movie studio with cousin Max,
Rebecca finds herself in front of the camera!

Rebecca to the Rescue
A day at Coney Island brings more
excitement and thrills than Rebecca expected.

Changes for Rebecca
When Rebecca sees injustice around her, she
takes to the streets and speaks her mind.